I LOVE YOU LIKE
YELLOW

For Michael
— A.B.

For Leah Alana and Vicki
—V.H.

I LOVE YOU LIKE YELLOW

words by **Andrea Beaty**   pictures by **Vashti Harrison**

Abrams Books for Young Readers
NEW YORK

I love you like yellow.

I love you like green.

Like flowery orchid

and sweet tangerine.

I love you like silly.

I love you like mad.

Like joyous and jolly.

Like silent and sad.

Like crunchy and crispy.

Like sweet and like tart.

I love you like crazy

with all of my heart.

I love you like slowly.

I love you like fast.

I love you like first,

and I love you like last.

Like brisk and like breezy.

Like bouncy and bold.

I love you like new,

and I love you like old.

I love you like stormy.

Like starry. Like still.

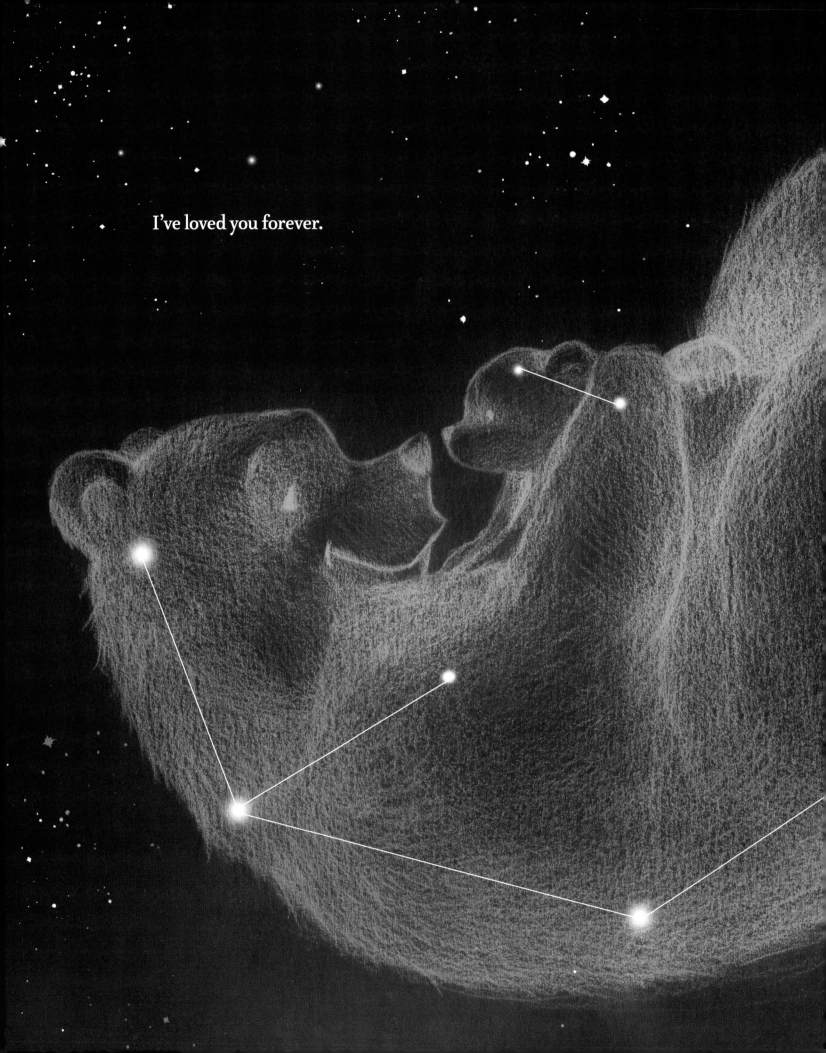

I've loved you forever.

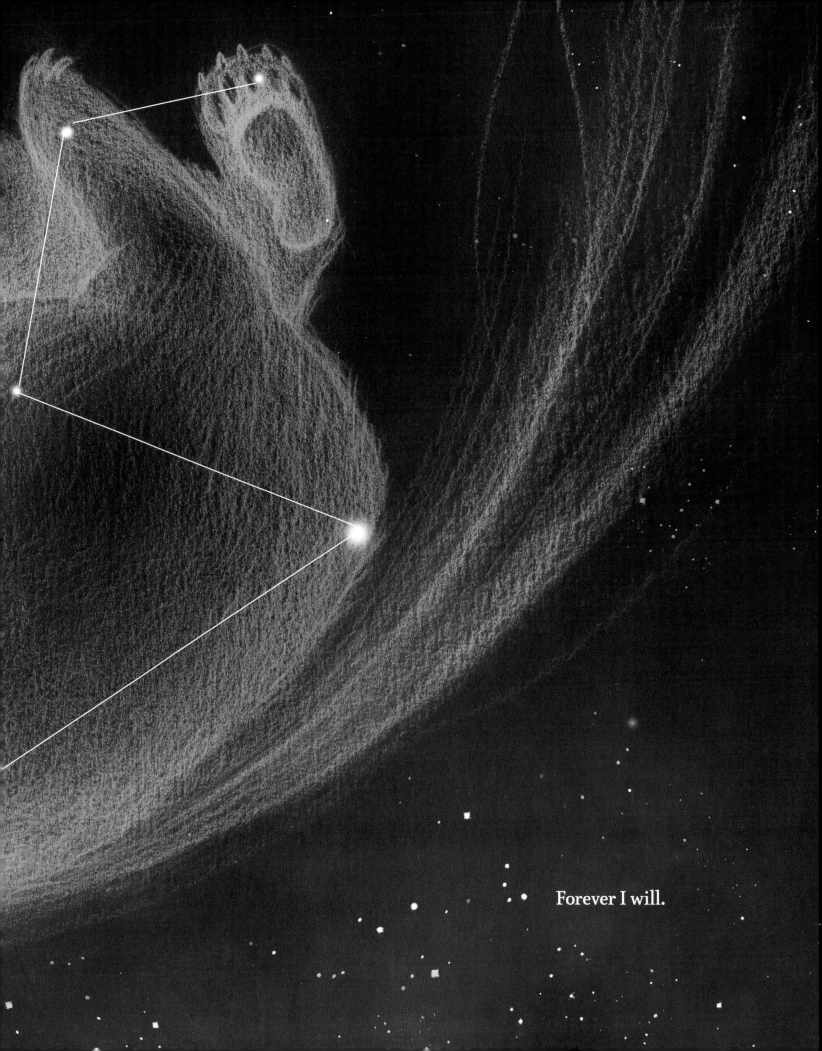

Forever I will.

Like sunny.

Like shady.

Like gloomy.

Like gray.

From the breaking of dawn

till the end of the day.

I love you, my dear one,

like that and like this—

drifting to sleep

with a hug and a kiss.

The illustrations in this book were created with colored pencil and Photoshop.

Cataloging-in-Publication Data has been applied for and may be obtained
from the Library of Congress.

ISBN 978-1-4197-4807-3

Text © 2022 Andrea Beaty
Illustrations © 2022 Vashti Harrison
Book design by Pamela Notarantonio

Printed and bound in China
10 9 8 7 6 5 4 3 2 1

Abrams Books for Young Readers are available at special discounts when purchased
in quantity for premiums and promotions as well as fundraising or educational
use. Special editions can also be created to specification. For details, contact
specialsales@abramsbooks.com or the address below.

Abrams® is a registered trademark of Harry N. Abrams, Inc.

ABRAMS The Art of Books
195 Broadway, New York, NY 10007
abramsbooks.com